[redacted]

TEEN
HOT LINE

RACISM

Ann T. Keene

RSVP
RAINTREE
STECK-VAUGHN
PUBLISHERS
The Steck-Vaughn Company

Austin, Texas

Consultants:
Nate Terrell, ACSW, Director of Counseling Services, Family Counseling Services, Camden, NJ
Rose Miller, Rose Miller Associates, Philadelphia, PA

Developed for Steck-Vaughn Company by Visual Education Corporation, Princeton, New Jersey
Project Director: Paula McGuire
Editors: Jewel Moulthrop, Linda Perrin
Photo Research: Sara Matthews

Raintree Steck-Vaughn Publishers staff
Editor: Kathy Presnell
Project Manager: Julie Klaus
Electronic Production: Scott Melcer
Photo Editor: Margie Foster

Library of Congress Cataloging-in-Publication Data
Keene, Ann T.
Racism / Ann T. Keene.
p. cm. — (Teen hot line)
Includes index.
ISBN 0-8114-3815-5
1. Racism—United States—Juvenile literature. 2. United States—Race relations—Juvenile literature. 3. Minorities—United States—Social conditions—Juvenile literature. I. Title. II. Series.
E184.A1K34 1995
305.8′00973 — dc20 94-30540
CIP
AC

Photo Credits: Cover: © Park Street; **15** © Tony Freeman/PhotoEdit; **21** © Mary Kate Denny/PhotoEdit; **31** UPI/Bettmann; **38** © Shirley Zeiberg; **41** Reuters/Bettmann; **44** © Richard Hutchings/PhotoEdit; **53** © Shirley Zeiberg; **57** © Jean-Marc Giboux/Gamma Liaison; **62** © Mark Morrison/Shooting Star; **66** © Michael Newman/PhotoEdit; **73** © Mary Kate Denny/PhotoEdit.

Printed and bound in the United States

1 2 3 4 5 6 7 8 9 0 LB 99 98 97 96 95

CONTENTS

What the Teen Hot Line Is All About

This book is like a telephone hot line. It answers questions about racism that may puzzle you. Answering your questions requires us to give you the facts about racism. You can use these facts to help you form your own attitudes. Think of us as the voice on the phone, there to answer your questions, even the ones that are hard to ask.

Today's teens are faced with some difficult challenges concerning racism. Just so you know where we stand, here is a list of what we think teens should do when they or someone they know is affected by racist attitudes:

1. Find out everything that you can about racism by reading this book and other books on the topic. Look for discussions of racism in newspapers and magazines, and watch TV programs and movies that have racism as their theme.

2 Talk with others to get more information. Discuss racism with friends, brothers and sisters, parents, and any other relatives. Discuss your concerns with other adults in whom you can confide, especially teachers, school counselors, and community social or religious leaders you know.

3 Be aware that many racist actions are illegal. There are local, state, and national laws that protect residents against racial discrimination in housing, employment, education, and recreation.

4 Know that judgments made about anyone only on the basis of race are wrong, whether those judgments are negative or positive.

5 Understand that racism comes from fear and can lead to more fear.

6 Become more aware of racism in your daily life, take a stand against it, and decide what steps you can take to help combat it. If someone indicates racist attitudes in your presence:

■ Let that person know you find such attitudes offensive.

■ Provide the person with the appropriate information to counteract existing stereotypes or erroneous beliefs about other races or groups.

■ Ask the person where he or she obtained racist attitudes and why he or she holds on to them.

■ Tell the person how hurtful these attitudes are to the people they are directed toward.

Interview

Bill is a 40-year-old African American dentist who lives in the midsize Ohio city where he grew up. He practices dentistry in his old neighborhood. Bill and his family were the first African Americans to live in that neighborhood, which was then mostly Italian. He became the first African American student in the local elementary school and later at what had been an all-white, private high school. In this interview, Bill describes his experiences as an African American in an all-white environment.

It may sound strange, but I really had no awareness of being "different" till I was about nine. I had a close friend then who was my age, an Italian kid. We hung out a lot together, played ball, rode our bikes in the neighborhood. I remember realizing for the first time that here was someone who looked different from me, had different skin color, different hair. Yet I didn't connect that difference with anything good or bad. It was just the way we were. We liked ourselves, and we liked each other.

Racism? I'm sure it was present in my community in some form or another. But it was never an active, obvious thing. I think it was probably more casual, the sort of thing you generally aren't aware of when you're little. I do have an early memory of my older brother coming home one day from school, crying because some kid had made a remark about his dark color. I must have been four or five, and he was five years older. I remember my mother taking him in her arms to comfort him, telling him he had beautiful skin. When my dad came home that evening, he went to the family of the kid who'd taunted my brother and talked to them.

And I have another memory—of the first time I heard the word "nigger." When I was ten, a white kid in the neighborhood had his bike stolen by some black kids who lived in another part of the city. The white kid was mad, and he just exploded with anger. "I'm gonna go down there and beat those niggers to a pulp," he said. I felt puzzled, not hurt. I guess I felt too good about myself to realize that the kid was hurling a racial insult that extended to me.

My parents had had a rough time growing up in the Deep South in the 1920s and 1930s. Racism was everywhere: Jim Crow laws kept African Americans poor and powerless. Lynchings were commonplace. In the late 1940s, my mom and dad got married and moved north to the small industrial city where I still live. They were looking for a better life for themselves and the family they wanted to raise, and I think they found it.

As you grow up, you gradually become more aware of what's going on around you. At the age of nine, I didn't think a whole lot about race, but my awareness grew rapidly after that. Why? Well, it was the 1960s, the time of the biggest civil rights movement in American history. You couldn't help knowing about it from the newspapers, from TV news. My father and mother talked to us kids about what it meant. It was deliverance, they said, from years of pain and turmoil. Laws were being passed that would finally make all black people the equal of all white people.

My parents never dwelled on the terrors of their early life. They didn't fill us with any of the poison of hate and resentment. And when the civil rights movement of the 1960s began to bring about positive changes in the lives of African Americans, my parents saw it in religious terms.

As far back as I can remember, our family belonged to a black Baptist church in another neighborhood, a neighborhood where only blacks lived. Yes, there was segregation in the North, too, but I only came to realize it later, much later. It was part of that growing awareness I spoke about earlier, an awareness of the world beyond your immediate family and neighborhood as you grow older. The church was at the center of our lives, and the Christian teachings, such as the Golden Rule, were reinforced by my parents: "Always treat everyone the way you yourself want to be treated."

My parents admired the nonviolent resistance of Dr. King. There was strength in dignity, they said. Indeed, for us kids, they were models of that dignity. I saw my parents' behavior in the outside world: at work, at church, in stores, at my school when they came to see us perform or to talk to our teachers. I saw them handle themselves with a confident dignity. By their own behavior, they showed us how to behave.

In particular, I watched my father closely, because that's who I wanted to be like when I grew up. I watched him in so many situations—being tactful, diplomatic, joking, even being angry when the situation called for it. He always carried himself with an air of self-control, and yet he always seemed natural, never stiff or reserved. He refused to let his emotions make him behave in an undignified manner.

We had a small, inexpensive record player in our home. It was mostly used by us kids to play our own records, but one day my dad brought home a recording of Dr. King's "I have a dream" speech, the one he made at the Lincoln Memorial in 1963. He played it for us. We all knew what it meant; we felt what it meant. Dr. King was looking ahead to a time when racism would disappear from the face of the Earth. My parents always believed that time would come, and they passed on that optimism to their children.

As a teenager, I won a scholarship to a private Catholic high school in the city. I was the first black student at the school. There was a lot of pressure, academic and social, but I don't remember ever feeling overwhelmed by it. I quickly made friends with a white guy, a basketball player like me. We were good athletes and played both junior varsity and varsity ball. I remember only one player on my team who gave me some trouble. He was someone who just couldn't accept a black player. But it may have been jealousy as much as racism: he just wasn't very good. He didn't make the varsity team.

A few times there were "racial incidents" when we played games at other high schools. I can remember once hearing some guy in the stands yell, "Hey, go after the spook—the spook's your man!" It made me want to play even harder, made me want to win just to spite him.

But not everybody can take it. During my four years at

the high school, several other black guys were admitted. The pressure was too much for them, and they dropped out. It was probably a combination of things, not just racist attitudes, but they couldn't take being in a mainly white school.

What helped me, in addition to sports and my family and friends, was the help I got from teachers—white teachers. I never had any black teachers growing up. Only as I grew older did I begin to realize that I hardly ever saw any African American professionals. I knew they were out there somewhere—my parents told me—but in an all-white neighborhood, they were invisible to me. That may have been one reason why I decided early on that I wanted a professional career.

Anyway, these white teachers in high school, one man in particular, gave me books to read about my race: *The Autobiography of Malcolm X*, Eldridge Cleaver's *Soul on Ice*. This was the late 1960s, when the black power movement was in full swing. Dr. King's nonviolence had been replaced by riots and slogans like "Burn, baby, burn." Here was all this unchanneled anger, rage, exploding in destructive ways. I knew that wasn't the way for me. Yes, I felt anger, too, when I didn't think progress for my race was happening fast enough. But I wanted to turn my anger into something positive, put it to good use.

I went to a small liberal arts college in my home state. There were only a few black students there, but I socialized with both blacks and whites. There were only two blacks in the pre-med program, and both of us went on to graduate programs at the state university. Each of us was the only black in the class: she in the medical school, and I in the dental school. Weren't there other qualified blacks who should have been accepted, too? Yes, I think there probably were.

But I don't think affirmative action is the answer. I don't believe in any kind of quota system. It's just as racist to favor blacks solely on the basis of skin color as it is to favor whites. I'm proud of what I accomplished. I got good grades and had high admissions test scores. I worked hard in college and in dental school.

And it paid off. The best reward to me is the satisfaction of knowing I'm good at what I do—and that what I do makes a difference. After I graduated from dental school, I came back to my old neighborhood to practice. Presenting myself as a product of the neighborhood is something I take great pride in. I'm giving something back to the place that nurtured me. It's a lot more integrated now, I'm happy to say. And when I see the variety of patients in my waiting room—black, white, rich, poor, the guy with the six-figure income sitting next to the single mother—this is what gives my life meaning.

BULLETIN BOARD

During World War II (1939–1945), the Nazi German government under Adolf Hitler killed 6 million Jews in an attempt to create a racially "pure" Aryan nation.

In April 1915, an estimated 600,000 Armenians were massacred by Turks.

During the 1930s, Soviet Union dictator Joseph Stalin was responsible for the murder of an estimated 10 million Ukrainians.

Between 1882 and 1925 there were at least 3,783 lynchings in the United States; most of the victims were black men, women, and children.

During World War II, some 120,000 Japanese Americans—more than two-thirds of them native-born American citizens—were moved from the West Coast into relocation camps, where some of them remained for almost four years.

The Los Angeles County Commission on Human Relations reported an increase in racially motivated hate crimes following the Los Angeles riots of 1992.

According to a research report by the Southern Poverty Law Center, there were 346 white supremacy groups in the United States in 1992, 27 percent more than there were in 1991.

In a survey of 550 editors of U.S. college newspapers, 49 percent reported race relations on their campuses as "fair" or "poor."

75 percent of the editors surveyed said that self-segregation by blacks on campus was common.

37 percent of the editors reported that blacks on their campuses believe that white students are "hostile and aloof."

24 percent of the editors reported that whites on their campuses were afraid of being physically attacked by black students.

According to a recent study by the U.S. Department of Housing and Urban Development (HUD), one-third of blacks live in neighborhoods that are 90 percent or more black; nearly two-thirds of all whites live in neighborhoods that are all or mostly white.

Another recent HUD study shows that whites are five times more likely to receive home-buying loans than blacks with similar incomes.

Median family income for blacks is more than 40 percent lower than median family income for whites.

In 1990, the median family income for Hispanics was $25,064, more than $10,000 lower than the median family income of $35,225 for all Americans.

Just over 2 of every 10 Hispanic families were living in poverty in 1990, compared with fewer than 1 of every 10 non-Hispanic families.

Sources:

Encyclopedia Britannica, 15th edition, 1994.

1994 Information Please Almanac.

The New York Times, May 14, 1994.

Bridges and Boundaries: African Americans and American Jews. George Braziller, 1992.

Los Angeles County Commission on Human Relations.

Anti-Defamation League of B'nai B'rith.

Southern Poverty Law Center.

"Race on Campus," *U.S. News and World Report*, April 19, 1993.

U.S. Department of Housing and Urban Development.

U.S. Department of Labor.

CHAPTER 1

Communicating

Q The black kids at school stick to themselves and don't want to mix with whites. It seems like they make a point of dressing differently, talking in a different way, and acting aloof toward the rest of the kids. I feel bad about this and would like to understand more about why this happens. I guess they think everybody else is racist, but aren't they racist, too?

A Let's begin by trying to understand what racist behavior is and what it isn't. Dressing and talking a certain way and sticking together in a group doesn't make the black kids racist. That kind of behavior is typical of almost all teenagers. Hanging out with people who are like themselves is something teens just like to do. Don't the white kids at your school form their own special groups, too?

Q Sure. There are the jocks, the "artsies," who put on the plays, and the "brainiacs," who can probably build their own computers. And kids from these different groups may not be real friendly with each other, but they aren't hostile either. The black kids are something else. I can't understand where they're coming from. Isn't it racist to act like they're so special and better than the rest of us?

A If the black kids are really saying they're better than whites, then yes, that is racist. And the kind of black separatism you're talking about—blacks deliberately

These white teenagers enjoy hanging out with people like themselves. When the whites stick to themselves, many African Americans feel they are being treated as inferiors.

and angrily separating themselves from whites—is happening in high schools and colleges across the country in the 1990s. Many blacks say that they are behaving this way in response to white racism.

• • • • • • • • • • • •

Racism is based on the belief that human beings can be divided into races and that some races are superior to others. *Racists* are people who believe that their own race is better than the others either mentally, morally, physically, or culturally and believe that this supposed advantage gives them license to dominate others. Today, social scientists believe there is no scientific evidence to support the idea that some people are superior or inferior to others, no matter how they may differ in groups or as individuals. People from all different races share the same essential qualities of all human beings. Every person, no matter what his or her race, is capable of thinking, reasoning, and feeling.

Q But black kids still seem different somehow. They talk differently, they like different kinds of music. Aren't those racial differences?

A People reflect the environment they come from, their family and community, their customs and speech, all of which have been influenced by many things, such as geographical location, history, or the way they have been treated by others. So people generally act the way the people around them do, but not because of inborn racial differences.

Q If that's true, why are people racist?

A There is a long history of racism throughout the world. People have tried to justify wars, slavery, genocide (mass murder), segregation, and discrimination by claims of racial superiority. Only during the twentieth century has the validity of racial theory been questioned, and even today people are debating how to deal with it in a multiracial society. Racism, after all, is the basis of prejudice. Many people have grown up thinking their way of appearing or acting is the best way and that, therefore, other ways are inferior.

You've probably heard this from your parents and teachers many times, but it's worth repeating: when people act superior to others, their actions often reflect what is actually a low self-image. By claiming to be better in some way than other people, they hide their true feelings and their own sense of inadequacy. It's a common emotional reaction, and sometimes it can be a very powerful one.

When something goes wrong in our lives, we often get angry, and we blame someone else for our troubles. We don't stop to find out the facts; we just react to hurt.

Q Are you saying that the black kids show hostility because they're blaming whites for their problems?

A It's more likely that they're assuming whites don't like *them.* They're protecting themselves, because they don't want to be hurt.

Q But the white kids I know have never done anything to the black kids. Why should the black kids be so angry with them?

A Everybody is aware that racism exists in the United States. It has been aimed mainly at blacks but also at Native Americans, Mexican Americans, Puerto Ricans, and other minorities, such as Asians and Jews. Sadly, by the time African American children reach adolescence, nearly all of them have had at least one racist experience. Maybe they were taunted on the playground because of their skin color. Or they might have heard an adult, a teacher maybe, make a negative remark about their race or group.

Whichever way it comes about, blacks quickly "get the message" that they're considered inferior by many whites. Black psychologists Kenneth and Mamie Clark have done many studies of black children. In one of their most famous studies in the 1940s, they gave black children a choice of white or black dolls when given instructions such as "Give me the doll that looks bad" or "Give me the doll that has the nice color." A large majority of the children preferred the white dolls. The Clarks were showing that the children felt society preferred white people.

Researchers Darlene and Derek Hopson repeated the experiment in 1985 and found that almost the same number of children chose white dolls as had chosen them in the experiment decades earlier. In an effort to change the children's view of the dolls—and of themselves—the Hopsons spoke well of the black dolls and read stories about black children that treated them positively. When the Hopsons ran the experiment again, a majority of the black children chose the black dolls. The Hopsons concluded that the children's self-esteem could be improved by constantly reinforcing a positive idea of black people.

By the time they're teenagers, most blacks believe that white people look down on them. Like teenagers of all races, black teens are trying to find out who they are and how they fit into the larger world. They're trying to discover what makes them unique—and at the same time, they're trying to battle racial discrimination. Like all teenagers, they're looking for comfort and reassurance and thus, choose to hang out with people like themselves. In addition, they're seeking a racial identity as a way of creating self-esteem.

Q I'm afraid there's going to be so much separation that the situation might turn violent. Is there anything my friends and I can do to make the situation better?

A Have you ever tried talking to the black kids?

Q Are you kidding? Just walk up to them and start a conversation? I'd be scared to death.

A You mean physically afraid? They're probably just as afraid of you as you are of them.

Q Yeah, maybe a little bit of the fear is physical. But I think what my friends and I are more afraid of is that we'll look, well, you know, kind of stupid. How do you start talking to someone who's a stranger to you?

A Not all the black kids are total strangers, are they? Don't you have classes with some of them?

Q Well, yes.

A Don't you ever sit near them?

Q Sometimes. Usually we just try to ignore each other.

A But if you want to understand somebody better and improve communication, you're going to have to try acting in a friendly way. Make friendly small talk about the class you're in together. Remember that if you act friendly toward other people, they're likely to act friendly in return.

All communication among human beings begins with a friendly overture. It also begins with a sense of mutual respect. When people feel valued, their self-esteem rises. As people start to feel more comfortable with one another, all students will feel less threatened and hostile.

Q Don't those kids have to make an effort, too?

A Yes—but remember that the black kids are a minority in your school. They already feel that they probably aren't wanted there—that's what their behavior is showing you. Put yourself in their position: how would you feel if you attended a school where the overwhelming majority of students were black? Would you feel like taking the first step?

Q No, I'm pretty sure I wouldn't. I know I'd feel dumb.

A One way to avoid "feeling dumb" is to have a clearer idea of what it is that blacks are facing, not just in your school but in society in general. Knowing a few facts may make you more sensitive to their feelings.

African Americans and other minorities experience discrimination in nearly every area of their lives. For example:

■ According to the U.S. Department of Housing and Urban Development (HUD), at least 2 million minorities are the victims of housing discrimination every year.

■ Another recent study by HUD shows that blacks and other minorities have more than a 50 percent chance of being discriminated against when looking for housing.

■ According to the 1990 census, 43 percent of blacks lived in homes they either owned or were buying, compared with 68 percent for whites. The median value of homes owned by blacks was $50,700, compared with $80,200 for homes owned by whites.

■ According to a study by the U.S. Department of Justice, blacks and other minorities have been the targets of more than 5,000 hate crimes during the past decade.

■ The overall rate of unemployment for blacks is more than twice that for whites. Within specific age groups, the rate is even higher. Among black males aged 16 to 19, for example, 42 percent were unemployed in 1992, compared to only 18.4 percent of whites.

■ In 1989, 45 percent of black female householders and 11 percent of black married-couple families were poor. These family types accounted for 94 percent of all poor black families. The corresponding figures for white families were significantly lower: 23 percent and 5 percent.

The poor economic and social condition of many African Americans has increased in recent years. One major reason is that jobs for less-skilled workers have declined. However, America has a long history of racism (see Chapter 3), and this has been a major factor in keeping African Americans from achieving equally with whites.

What You Can Do

■ The most important thing for all of you—black, white, Hispanic, Asian, or someone from another group—is to understand what racism is and how it affects your lives. Discuss racism with your teachers and counselors. Ask them for their

The early high school years present a good opportunity to get to know groups of people who are different from your own group.

suggestions on how to improve race relations in your school.

■ Confront and examine your own beliefs and assumptions about other racial or cultural groups. People who have rid themselves of prejudices radiate a positive attitude of acceptance and happiness. This attitude can be infectious.

■ Learn to love and value yourself, since many prejudices stem from low self-esteem and the need to feel superior to others. Research has shown that people who feel positive about themselves have far fewer prejudices than those who do not.

■ Keep trying to become acquainted with new groups of people. If you find it is hard to approach someone you don't know well, find other kids to help you out. The people you are trying to get to know may be as shy in the situation as you are. You may have to try to talk to them more than once, so don't be discouraged if the first time isn't a great success.

■ Plan ahead. Work out a time when you and the person (or group) you wish to approach can meet easily and without awkwardness or strain. Know what you are going to say. Be positive, and listen carefully to what is said to you. Don't insist on a long discussion just yet, but be ready to answer any question about your intentions. Chances are, you've just taken the first step toward making a new friend, as well as putting an end to racism in your school or neighborhood.

CHAPTER 2

Minorities and Stereotypes

Q My name is Enrique. Things are pretty cool here for kids—I have lots of white friends in school. But sometimes I see teachers and the cops giving us Chicanos a hard time. Is there any way out of this?

A Incidents of bias or discrimination such as you mention happen all too often to minority groups in the United States. While the country is becoming more and more diverse, traditionally the benefits of society—education, jobs, leadership—have all been mostly geared toward whites. Racism is a way of life in America.

Stereotypes

And whether they're aware of it or not, many people—whites and members of other ethnic groups also—are affected by what we call stereotypes, oversimplified or standardized images about how a person or a group of people behave. Mexicans, for example, have been pictured as lazy peasants sleeping under a big sombrero, or as dangerous and violent desperados. Making general statements like these are as silly as saying all people with long hair use drugs or all African American people dance well.

Since many whites do not see themselves as members of a racial group (but simply as the standard against which other groups are compared), they are often surprised to learn that other racial groups have stereotypes about them. For example, many African Americans believe that white parents do not discipline their children properly.

Q I think I see what you mean here. If the cops have to break up fights with a bunch of Chicano kids a few times, they go ahead and act as if all Chicanos are troublemakers, whether they are or not.

A Unfortunately, yes. That's what sometimes happens. When someone seems "different" in some way, people become uncomfortable or even feel threatened. If people would take the time to find out something about the person, they would find that there's no reason for fear.

History and Discrimination: The First Americans

Racism has a long history in the United States, starting with the systematic near-destruction of the original Native American civilization that began with the coming of Europeans in the late 15th century. From that time, the Native Americans (called "Indians" by Columbus, who thought he was sailing in the Indian Ocean) faced enslavement, extermination, displacement to the West, or segregation in reservations by European settlers. Some estimates place the decline in the Native American population (in what is today the United States and Canada) from a high of about 2 to 3 million in 1492 to a low of 228,000 in 1890. This decline was accompanied by a loss of tribal land and authority, severe health problems, alcoholism, and poverty, problems that have only just begun to be addressed in this century.

Native Americans and the Constitution

The status of Native Americans was made clear by the Constitution, which established them as aliens, unable to be naturalized. In practice, by the mid-19th century, many states treated Native Americans as if they were citizens, but it was not until 1924 that Congress made all native-born American Indians citizens.

Chinese Americans

The first Chinese to come in numbers to America arrived following the discovery of gold in California in 1848. Some panned for gold, while others worked on the railroads, farmed, or became businesspeople. In the 1870s unemployment was high in California, and prejudice and fear of losing their jobs led many whites to mistreat the Chinese. In many places Chinese were beaten and their homes destroyed. Attempts were made to stop Chinese from immigrating to the United States, and the new California constitution stated that companies and local governments could not hire Chinese.

The Chinese Exclusion Act

In 1882, the U.S. Congress passed the Chinese Exclusion Act, which kept many Chinese workers and their wives from immigrating to the United States and from traveling freely back and forth to their home country. The Chinese Exclusion Act was not repealed until 1943, when attitudes changed because of Chinese American participation in World War II. Since then, the Chinese Communist takeover of mainland China and the Vietnam War complicated relations between Asians and Americans, but a new immigration law passed in 1965 proved fairer to Asians in general.

Prejudice and discrimination against Asians still exist. Some Asians feel that their drive to excel often causes resentments and unfair numbers of places in colleges. Other Asians suggest that they cannot compete with white Americans for jobs.

Other Immigrants

In the 19th century, and well into the 20th, American citizens treated newly arrived immigrants, such as the Irish and Italians, with contempt. Most of these immigrants were very poor and had left Europe because of famine and poverty. They found themselves near the bottom of the social ladder. They could hold only the lowliest jobs and were made to feel unwelcome in many other ways. They were being discriminated against by other Americans.

Americans found the customs and manners of the Irish and Italians strange, especially their ways of speaking and their Catholic religion, and they feared the new immigrants would

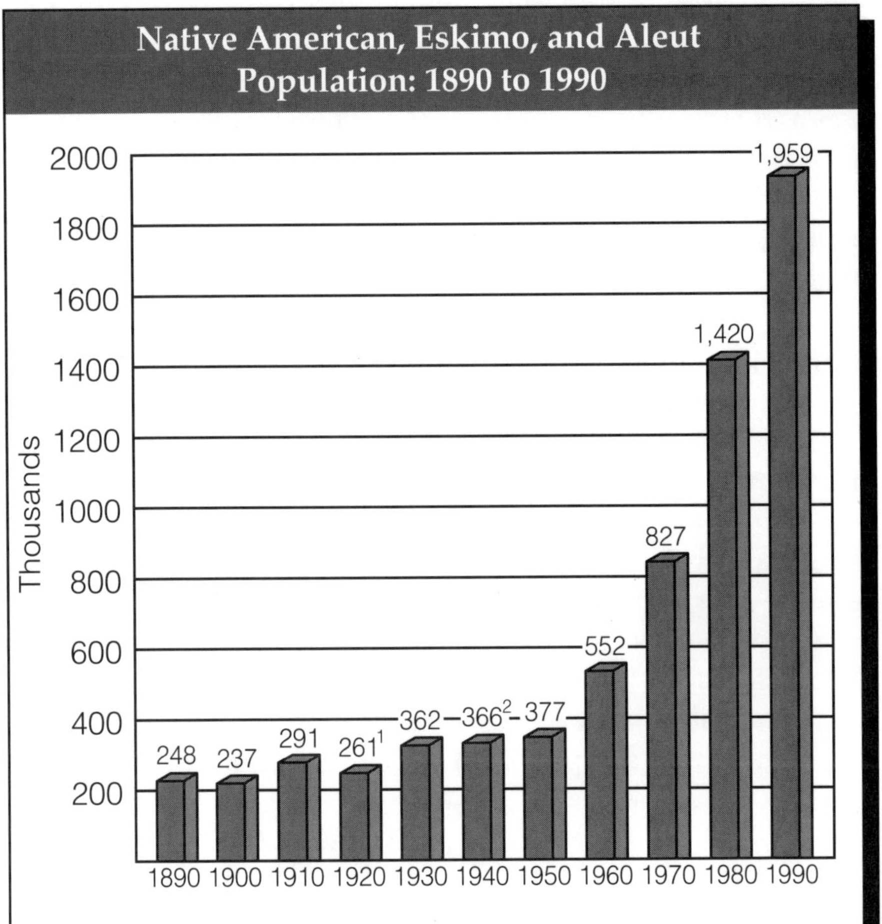

1 Partially estimated.
2 Eskimo and Aleut population are based on 1939 counts.
Source: Bureau of the Census

take their jobs away. They taunted the newcomers with derisive nicknames.

Over the years, the descendants of Irish and Italian immigrants gradually became accepted and assimilated into American society. Many of them rose to prominence in business, the arts, and politics.

Old and New Mexican Immigration

Many Mexican Americans belong to the oldest groups of immigrants. They are descendants of the first settlers in California and the Southwest. In 1848, some 85,000 Mexicans lived in the territories newly won by the United States as a result of war and annexation. By treaty, many were given the right to stay in the United States and were promised all the rights of U.S. citizens. All too soon, however, the treaty was ignored, and former Mexicans lost their lands to rich and greedy white Americans.

Mexicans have continued to come to the United States in the 20th century and are counted among the newest wave of Hispanic peoples, who also come from Puerto Rico and Latin America. According to the 1990 census, there were 22.4 million Hispanics in the United States; of these 13.7 million, almost 9 percent of the nation's 250 million people, were of Mexican birth or ancestry.

No Change in Treatment

Mexican Americans have been dispossessed of their lands and discriminated against in employment, housing, and education wherever they live in the West and Southwest. At first, many worked in agricultural jobs and lived in poverty in rural areas. Now most Mexican Americans live in cities and work in factories, stores, and offices. Many entered the country illegally, without documentation. They are resented by some people who think "illegals" take jobs from other Americans, keep wages low, and put a strain on social services, such as schools, hospitals, and welfare. However, these Mexicans pay taxes and Social Security and spend money in the United States.

A great disparity exists between conditions along the Mexican American border, with lower prices for most goods and services on the Mexican side and higher wages and more

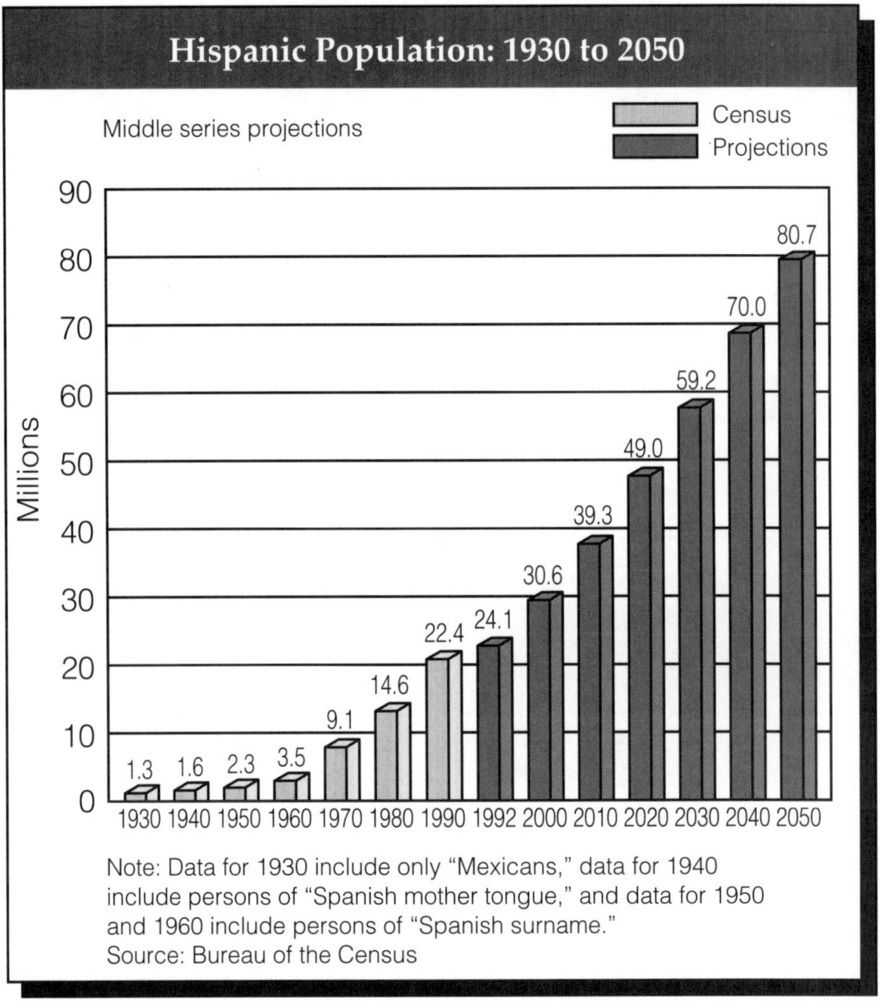

The Hispanic population grew over 7 times as fast as the rest of the nation between 1980 and 1990. The Census Bureau's projections suggest that this rapid growth may continue into the 21st century.

jobs on the American side. As long as this is so, Mexicans will continue to be attracted to the United States and will come either as temporary or permanent residents. And unless attitudes change, they will remain poor and discriminated against.

Changing Attitudes

Q Yeah, like me and some of my friends. If we walk in a group in the halls, the teachers on duty keep an eye on us, like we're going to start something. And when we're just hanging out in the park or shooting baskets, the cops keep driving by. That doesn't happen to white kids. How can we get people to stop judging us as bad?

A Well, maybe you and your friends should speak to the teachers and the cops and ask them to explain why you are treated this way. You might ask for a meeting with your teachers first. You can explain to them that their actions make you feel put down, seem unfair, and contribute to overall racial unease in the school. You might suggest trying to work with them to improve the situation. You could then ask for their help in explaining your feelings to the police. With the teachers on your side, you'd have some help in changing the attitudes of the police and be on your way to making a difference in the whole community.

Q Do you really think they'd listen to us?

A Yes, I do. I believe that if you guys work out a strategy in advance and make your plans carefully, you could bring about a lot of change around here. You would not be the first Mexican Americans to do so.

You know, I am very impressed by the fact that you

can speak another language and know firsthand another historical tradition. I'm sure that your teachers are impressed, too, and would be delighted to encourage others to get to know you and to respect your rights. A lot of people from the majority culture in the United States are becoming more interested in the cultural traditions of Hispanics and other minority groups and are recognizing the significant contributions members of these groups have made to American society.

Numerous Mexican American men and women have left their mark on American tradition, some of them wishing to bring about a change in attitudes, just like you. Take, for example, the stories of Cesar Chavez and Henry Cisneros.

Cesar Chavez

Cesar Chavez was born into a Mexican American family in Yuma, Arizona, in 1927. His parents were migrant farm workers, and Chavez had only a little formal education. He dropped out of school in seventh grade to work full-time in the fields. He served in the U.S. Navy during World War II, and after his discharge in 1947, he became a migrant worker again. In 1952, Chavez became a member of a self-help community organization. He led voter registration drives and helped Mexican Americans with immigration problems. He saw that migrant workers had a tough life and understood that, because most workers were immigrants, Americans found it easy to ignore their problems.

In 1962, Chavez founded the National Farm Workers Association and was able to negotiate a few pay raises from growers. In 1965, he joined with another farm workers' union to become the United Farm Workers and got help from other labor unions across the country to organize a strike. At that time farm workers made less than $2,000 a year, worked long hours, and had no health or unemployment insurance.

Using nonviolence and other tactics of the civil rights movement then in full swing, Chavez struck the major grape growers in California. Unable to stop them from hiring other Mexican farm workers to harvest their grapes and from shipping the grapes out of state for sale, Chavez organized a

Showing solidarity against grape growers, Cesar Chavez (front row left), head of the United Farm Workers Union, and Walter Reuther (front row center, holding Huelga sign), president of the United Auto Workers, lead a group of striking pickets in Delano, California, in December, 1965.

national boycott of all California table grapes. The strike lasted five years, ending in 1970 with a labor contract with the growers, who had been badly hurt by the boycott. The workers received a wage increase and provisions for health insurance.

In 1977, the United Farm Workers made an agreement with other large table grape growers and began the long fight to represent farm workers in negotiating with the growers of other crops.

Chavez died in 1993, a nationally celebrated and beloved figure.

Henry Cisneros

Henry Cisneros was born in San Antonio, Texas, in 1947. His father was descended from early Spanish settlers in the American Southwest. His mother was the daughter of a revolutionary journalist who fled dictatorship in Mexico, settled in San Antonio, and became a staunch backer of Mexican American activities.

Henry grew up in a large, industrious family and attended Catholic schools. He graduated from Texas A&M University with a degree in city management in 1968. He worked for the Model Cities program for urban revitalization in San Antonio and had his first view of problems between the city's established Anglo leaders and its poor Mexican majority.

Cisneros earned an M.A. degree in urban planning at Texas A&M in 1970. The next year he became a White House fellow in Washington, D.C., in a program started under the administration of Lyndon Johnson. The program allowed young people who hoped to work in government to have an opportunity to serve as assistants to members of the cabinet or the White House staff. Cisneros served under Elliott Richardson, the secretary of health, education, and welfare. Cisneros earned another M.A. in public administration from the John F. Kennedy School of Government at Harvard University in 1973, was a teaching assistant at the Massachusetts Institute of Technology (MIT), and then returned home to teach at the

University of Texas in San Antonio. In 1975, he received his Ph.D. in public administration from George Washington University.

At age 27, only months after he returned to his home city, Cisneros was elected to the city council. He worked hard on projects that would benefit both Mexican Americans and the city as a whole. In 1981 he became mayor, the first Mexican American to be elected mayor of San Antonio since 1842 and the first Hispanic American to be elected mayor of a large American city. Repeatedly re-elected mayor, Cisneros worked hard for San Antonio's growth and prosperity and succeeded in relieving the tensions between Anglos and Chicanos and in building a solid partnership for change.

In 1993, President Bill Clinton named Cisneros to his cabinet as secretary of housing and urban development (HUD).

What You Can Do

Cesar Chavez and Henry Cisneros are outstanding representatives not only of Mexican Americans but also of all Americans who strive to improve the lives of those around them. You may not be able to follow directly in their footsteps, but learning about their lives will help focus your attention on the many problems facing minorities in America today. Do some further reading about the history of Mexican Americans and compare it with the history of other immigrant groups in America. You'll find many similarities among them, and you may develop new understanding for events happening today.

You may also find some practical suggestions. Many immigrants created social clubs and organizations to help one another. You may find some new and exciting ways to strengthen your ties to your culture and your people.

Q A couple of my friends and I already belong to a Chicano social club. I bet there are some things we could do to help Chicanos at my school, like organizing a tutoring program for some of the newer kids who need to learn English. Do you think the school would go for that?

A I'll bet the teachers need all the help they can get. You might also suggest working with teachers on an assembly program for the whole school in which Mexican Americans, African Americans, and other groups present information about their cultures. You could then divide up into smaller, culturally diverse groups to discuss different students' experiences with discrimination and prejudice.

You could also think about ways to become active in your community and try to change negative stereotypes. You say Chicanos have a negative image where you live because a few Chicano kids keep getting into trouble. Maybe you can change that image by organizing a group of volunteers somewhere, like at soup kitchens and homeless shelters. They can always use extra hands.

What Else You Can Do

You said earlier that sometimes you think the teachers at your school come down too hard on Chicanos. But don't make the same mistake that you think they're making—don't assume that all the teachers are prejudiced just because you've seen a few acting that way.

■ Try talking to a counselor you like at your high school about this. Ask for suggestions about improving relationships between teachers and students.

■ You might also want to speak to teachers directly. Choose a teacher you're friendly with and admire. Tell him or her that you're concerned about how minorities in your school are treated. Your teacher may not be aware of the difficulties you and your friends are having.

■ Explain to the teacher that you would like to find ways to create positive images for Mexican Americans and other minorities in your school. Ask for advice on how to counter stereotypes that teachers may have.

■ Find out what organizations exist in your community to counter prejudice. Many city and town governments have human rights commissions or other official groups that work to overcome discrimination. In particular, these groups often handle complaints about police behavior toward minorities. Ask your local human rights organization what it is doing to help Mexican Americans fight prejudice in your community.

■ Talk to your friends about your concerns—all your friends, Chicanos and non-Chicanos alike. Always be on the lookout for ways to overcome stereotypes and prejudices—not only against Mexican Americans but against all races and all minority groups.

■ Talk to your parents about discrimination. If appropriate, ask them about their experiences as newly arrived immigrants in America. Find out what prejudice they have experienced, and how they are handling it. Together you may be able to think of other ways to overcome minority stereotypes in your own community.

■ Finally, be alert to daily incidents of discrimination. If, for example, you hear someone make a remark that stereotypes Chicanos or any other ethnic or racial group, let that person know how you feel about it. Don't get angry—voice your concern in a reasonable way. Explain that stereotypes are both false and unfair. Point out the positive contributions of individual Mexican Americans and other minorities.

A Dictionary of Racism

affirmative action: A policy to improve the educational and employment opportunities of individuals who have been discriminated against in the past—for example, members of minority groups, disabled persons, and women; affirmative action programs usually set aside a certain number, or quota, of positions for such individuals. Critics of affirmative action say that the policy is unfair because it causes reverse discrimination.

civil rights: In the United States, the right to live according to the liberties guaranteed under the U.S. Constitution; these include equal opportunity in education and employment and equal treatment under the law.

discrimination: Unjustifiable negative behavior directed at a person or a group, often based on prejudice.

prejudice: An opinion or "prejudgment" about another person or group that is not based on facts; prejudices are usually emotional reactions and are often made out of fear.

racism: The belief that human beings can be divided into races and that the members of some races are superior to others.

racists: People who believe in the doctrine of racism and believe that their race is superior.

stereotype: A generalized image of a race, an ethnic group, or any other specific group. Stereotypes ignore individual characteristics, are usually negative, and are often used to support feelings of prejudice.

CHAPTER 3

Reaching Out

Q We live in a mixed neighborhood. About a third of the people who live here are African American, but most of us are white. When I was really little, my parents didn't mind if I played with all the other kids. But now that we're older, my mom and dad want me to stay with my own kind. But I've got a couple of really good black friends. I don't want to break off with them. How can I talk my parents out of their attitude?

A Feelings and ideas about race run very deep, and it may be difficult to change your parents' attitudes. Apparently they felt it was okay to live together with more than one race all these years. They were not hostile to African Americans, and the African Americans were not hostile to the whites in the neighborhood. They probably had some casual friendly relationships as parents and thought it was great for the small children to play together.

Now that the children of both races are growing up, however, some repressed fears may be coming to the surface. The parents may be comparing the calm, friendly life in the neighborhood with the world outside. And what they see out there may make them feel cautious about the future and may make them want to protect their children from a place where different races do not, in general, live peacefully together.

Q Yeah, the funny thing is my black friends have told me the same thing about *their* parents. My friends' parents tell them that if they keep hanging out with me, they're going to think they can be like white people. They're going to forget that they're black. They're afraid that when their kids "act white" they'll be rejected by whites. Then nobody'll want to be friends with them, blacks or whites. What's going on?

A "What's going on" is racism, and it has been going on for a long time! It has indelibly printed itself on people's lives today and throughout American history.

Parents of different races and ethnic groups often encourage their children to play together when very young. When the kids get older, however, parents sometimes find themselves influenced by racist attitudes.

Racism Yesterday and Today

Racism in American society goes back to the 17th century, when slavery was first introduced into the American colonies. Over a period of nearly two centuries, millions of African men, women, and children were brought against their will to the New World.

The Legacy of Slavery

Throughout this time blacks were considered inferior and often treated cruelly. After the Civil War ended in 1865 and the slaves were freed, laws and amendments to the U.S. Constitution gave blacks the full rights of citizenship, including the right to vote. However, many white people still believed that African Americans were inferior to whites. These whites did not want to share schools, transportation, hospitals, and other public facilities with blacks, especially in the South (where the majority of black people in the United States lived until the early years of the 20th century). They required blacks to use segregated, or separate, facilities.

Long-established economic patterns kept African Americans in an inferior position in American society, in the North as well as in the South. Most black people were able to find work only as unskilled laborers, and throughout the country blacks were generally discouraged from trying to improve themselves through education.

Blacks Move North

In the early decades of the 20th century, large numbers of blacks began to move north to work in factories in major cities like Detroit, New York, and Chicago. Blacks had more civil rights in the North than they did in the South. They could usually vote, for example (in the South they were discouraged from voting, in various and sometimes violent ways), and they didn't have to use segregated public facilities. They could also attend public schools with white children—if they lived in the same neighborhood. But blacks generally lived with other blacks in the poorest areas of the city, areas known as slums.

Many blacks found that some northern white people disliked black people as much as some southern whites did. Some northern white people believed that blacks were taking jobs that belonged to whites. Tensions between whites and blacks often erupted in riots that killed many people and caused millions of dollars in property damage during the 1920s, 1930s, and 1940s.

The Coming of Civil Rights

Despite all these problems, many people worked for improvement in the lives of black people. The Reverend Martin Luther King, Jr., formed a coalition of blacks and whites that promised equality for everyone. Other black leaders formed more radical, separatist groups. Civil rights efforts included nonviolent protest marches and sit-ins, which sometimes resulted in violent reactions and confrontations with police. Federal laws were passed that made segregation in public schools, the armed forces, and housing illegal. In 1964, Congress passed the comprehensive Civil Rights Act that outlaws discrimination in many areas, including employment and public accommodations. And in 1965, Congress passed the Voting Rights Act, which increased the number of southern blacks able to register to vote.

The Legacy Lives On

While the civil rights struggle had left an enduring mark on American life, there was a decline in protest activity after the 1960s. Some forms of public discrimination against African Americans had come to an end, some black candidates were elected to public office, and antiblack violence in the South lessened. Despite these changes, however, as we have seen,

The civil rights movement of the 1960s joined both African Americans and whites in protest actions. Here, Dr. Martin Luther King, Jr., (center) and the Reverend Ralph Abernathy (with newspaper) lead 300 protest marchers from Selma to Montgomery, Alabama, in March 1965. Protest activities declined after the 1960s.

patterns of racism continue in the United States. In addition, nearly every day there are stories on television and the radio and in newspapers and magazines about racist incidents.

A Prom and a Protest

For example: In February 1994, the principal of an Alabama high school called a meeting of the juniors and seniors in advance of the prom. He asked how many planned to bring a date of a different race to the prom. Several people raised their hands, including Revonda Bowen, who planned to attend the prom with her white boyfriend. Revonda's father is white and her mother is black. When the principal saw the raised hands, he canceled the prom, saying he wanted to prevent anyone from getting hurt. When Revonda asked the principal whom she was supposed to go with, he replied, "That's the problem. Your mom and dad shouldn't have had you. You were a mistake." Revonda burst out crying, and her friends crowded around her in sympathy.

The Principal Backs Down

The next day, after several parents had complained, the principal reversed his decision and allowed the prom to go on. The school board suspended the principal (with pay), and a federal lawsuit was filed on behalf of Revonda against the school board and the principal for violating her civil rights. A separate protest prom was held the same night as the school prom, and when the principal was reinstated—never having apologized to Revonda, students boycotted the school.

Unfortunately, racist incidents like this continue to occur in the United States. Laws cannot quickly overturn centuries of ingrained prejudice.

What It Means

Q Are you trying to say my parents might be worried that I might *marry* a black person someday?

A I can't say whether they are or not, but until recently, there were still laws on the books in some places against mixed marriages, and a lot of people—both black and white—are still opposed to them. The thought of marriage between different races seems to bring up old taboos—or forbidden activities—that still frighten some people or remind others of inequalities between the races that have not been overcome.

Inequalities

What one can say for sure is that in the early 1990s, life for most African Americans continues to be worse in general than it does for white Americans. Here are just a few disturbing statistics:

	Whites	*Blacks*
Persons living below the poverty level (1991)	11.3%	32.7%
Infant mortality rate (1990)	7.6%	18.0%
Children living with mother only (1991)	17.0%	54.0%
High school graduates entering college (1992)	64.0%	49.0%

African Americans and others who expected great improvements to arise from the gains made through the civil rights movement in the 1960s have been sorely disappointed in the subsequent decades, as government expenditures have dropped and opportunities have faded away. Poverty, joblessness, and crime rates continue to plague the black community.

In schools and on college campuses, blacks and whites are carrying on separate lives, staying in their own groups and clubs, often living in separate residences, and rarely socializing with one another. It is a time of division between the races, some members of whom seem to have lost completely the will to work things out.

Keeping the Faith

Q This all sounds very discouraging. You know, my parents don't really dislike my black friends. "Just keep away from them," they keep saying. "Don't borrow trouble." That just seems crazy to me. Isn't there something we could do about this?

A What are your black friends doing about the pressure from their parents?

Q So far they're not paying attention. They say they like me too much to stop being friends. I think it's really great that we get along so well, but I'm beginning to wonder how long it can last.

A It sounds like you and your black friends have gotten past stereotypes. You've found out that most human beings have many more things in common than they have differences. Hang on to those convictions.

For teenagers who have grown up together as friends, the fact that they come from different races is unimportant. If you have no friends from another race, you may want to examine your feelings to find out why.

Here are some specific things you can do:

■ Remind your parents that they didn't tell you whom you could be friends with when you were a small child. They didn't separate you from the black children in your neighborhood. You were able to choose the friends you wanted to have.

■ Tell your parents how happy you are that they didn't raise you with racist attitudes. Describe to them how much it's meant to you to be able to make the friends you did.

■ Since your friends' parents are also giving them a hard time about keeping you as a friend, why not try getting all the parents together? Maybe you could take a stab at talking things through all together.

The Delany Sisters

Take a tip from the lives of two black women who are more than 100 years old. Sadie and Bessie Delany are sisters. They grew up in the South and later moved north for their education. One became a dentist and the other a schoolteacher at a time in the early 20th century when segregation and other forms of racism made it difficult for blacks to obtain a good education and have a professional career. For many years the sisters have lived together in Mount Vernon, an integrated suburb of New York City.

The sisters recently wrote their autobiography, *Having Our Say.* Their book has become very popular, and the sisters have received a lot of attention. They enjoy their new celebrity status, but they say that one thing above all has meant the most to them. For the first time, they are meeting their white neighbors. The sisters are pleased but feel rather sad because, "it took so long." The Delany sisters kept to themselves for so many years because they thought white people weren't interested in knowing *them.*

Interview

Mitsuko—"Mimi" to her friends—is a high school senior in a Chicago suburb. Her mother is a Japanese American; her father, whose ancestors immigrated to America from Ireland and Germany in the 19th century, is white. Race has always been an issue in the lives of Mitsuko and her family. In this interview she describes her experience growing up "between races," and the special pressures she's had to face.

For a long time, I really didn't think the words "racism" and "racist" had any connection to my life. Sure, I knew I was half Japanese. I also knew I looked so much like my mother that my friends had a hard time believing I wasn't all Japanese. But in the years since I was born (in 1976), I've always heard "racism" and "racist" used to describe discrimination against African Americans.

My grandfather died a few years ago, but my grandmother is still alive. When I was little, my grandparents didn't talk much about the past. I knew they'd moved to Chicago after World War II, but I didn't know why. My mother would only say there was a better job for her father there, but I don't think he liked working in a factory. He'd retired by the time I was born, but he always looked so sad, even when he worked in his little backyard garden.

I learned the full story only two years ago, after my grandfather died. I had to do a report in my American history class on World War II. We were all supposed to find someone in our family or neighborhood who'd been alive during the war and interview him or her. Well, my grandmother had just moved in with us, so I decided I would interview her. I sat down with Grandma and asked my questions.

It was pretty upsetting for her, but she answered all my questions. She told me how she and my grandfather had been forced to move to a resettlement camp in Utah in 1942. Soldiers had taken them and other Japanese by train to the camp. Because the United States was at war with Japan, the American government believed that Japanese living in this country couldn't be trusted. The U.S. government was afraid that the American Japanese would become spies for Japan.

My grandparents lived at the camp for nearly four years. Both of them worked at various jobs, mostly farming. They had to live in a barracks with other Japanese families. It was very crowded and noisy, my grandmother said, and they were very unhappy. The only good thing that happened, she said, was the birth of my mother, in 1944.

My grandmother said that after the war there was nothing to go back to in California. The government offered to resettle many of the Japanese held in camps, so she and my grandfather moved with my mother, who was two years old, to Chicago. Several of their friends moved there, too, but there was no Japanese neighborhood to welcome them, like the one in California. They and the other Japanese had to live in an all-black neighborhood on the South Side of Chicago.

Now this really shocked me. I never knew that Asians in the United States had been segregated like this. But my grandmother insisted it was true. "Ask your mother," she said.

Well, I did ask my mother. And she told me it was true. She also told me she didn't like me upsetting my grandmother with lots of questions about the past. "But you never told me all this," I said.

"I never told you because I didn't want to upset you," my mom said. "Besides, it's all in the past. What happened, happened. We can't do anything about it now."

But I don't agree with her. I think that even though our lives are much easier now, we should still remember the past and what it was like. Later on, when my mother was in a better mood, I got her to talk more about her childhood. I told her that it made me feel closer to her to know the truth. She opened up a bit then. She talked about how painful it was to live as one of three Japanese families in an otherwise all-black neighborhood.

"Why was it painful?" I asked. "Did the black people treat you badly?"

"Oh, no," she said. "Most of the black people accepted us. The white kids at the school we went to, they were the problem. They'd tease us, tell us we lived in Nigger Town."

Knowing all this really helped me understand my mother better. I've always thought she was too demanding. My father's more easygoing, and in many ways I take after him more. Despite my mother's sternness, I've never doubted for a minute that both my parents love me very much. I know that my father and mother are devoted to each other, and the respect they show each other is something I admire. When you see racial harmony in your own family, you know it's possible in the rest of the world.

Sometimes I wish my mother could laugh and relax more. Especially, I wish she wouldn't spend so much time worrying about me and my future. She always tells me that I've got to be the best at everything I do. But I guess that's natural: I'm her only surviving child. I had an older brother who died when I was six. As I read more about my mother's heritage, I realize that hard work and a strong family are the most important parts of Japanese life.

Our suburb is middle-class, with a sprinkling of some very rich and a few poor families. All the Asians—three Japanese families, one Korean, one Chinese—are professionals: doctors, a businessman, several professors. My father teaches English at the local community college.

I've never felt the racism that my mother and her parents had to live with, but there've been incidents one might call racist. The first one I remember happened in kindergarten. I was the only Asian in the class, and I must have looked strange to a lot of those kids. One little girl kept following me around the whole first day, just staring at me. Finally, she asked me point-blank what was wrong with my eyes!

Asian Population for Selected Groups: 1990

(percent distribution)

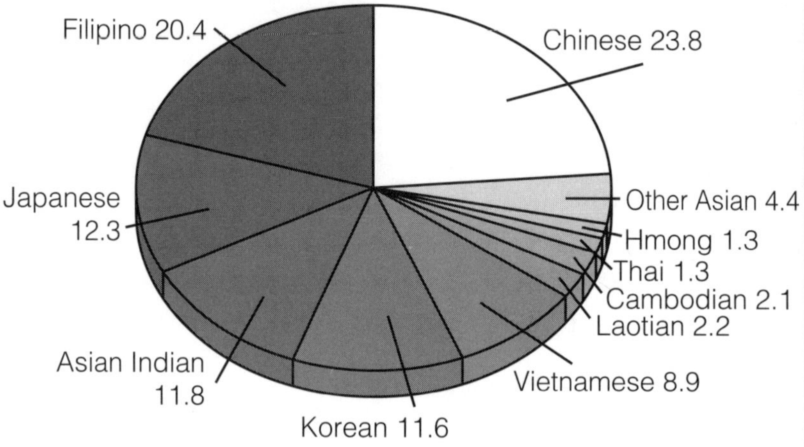

Source: Bureau of the Census

I thought something terrible had happened to my eyes. I had no idea she'd never seen an Asian person before. I burst into tears and ran to the teacher. The teacher was kind and knew how to handle the situation. She put her arms around me and told me I had perfectly fine big, brown eyes. And then she and her assistant sat all of us down in a circle and talked about how God had made different races. We looked different on the outside, the teacher said, but on the inside we were all the same.

It was a beautiful moment for me. I don't think I'll ever forget it.

There were other "incidents" as well. When people asked me what race I was and I said "half-Japanese," they almost always asked, "Which half?" They thought it was a joke, but I started to get really upset by it. My parents gave me some good advice. "You're not half anything," they said. "Tell them you're all-American."

People make dumb comments, and they always will, I guess. Sometimes they're funny, like when people blurt out, "Oh, you have a white father!" when they meet my family for the first time. My last name isn't Japanese, but I guess because I look just like my mother, they think I can't be white. And everybody assumes that I'm going to be the class brain just because I'm Asian.

I'm a good student, but sometimes I'd like to slide a bit, not worry about excelling and going to college. Both my parents tell me I should be proud of being smart, but frankly I get more pleasure from hanging out with my friends. Being liked and respected is one of the most satisfying feelings a person can have.

CHAPTER 4

Anti-Semitism

Q My name is Aaron. I try to get along with everybody, but the other day a boy at school told an anti-Semitic joke in my presence and thought it was funny. Since I'm Jewish, that really hurt me. Is there anything I can do about this?

A Unfortunately, anti-Semitic jokes—jokes that make fun of Jews—are all too common. Sometimes people deliberately tell these jokes because they are prejudiced against Jews. More often, however, jokes like these are repeated by people who should know better but just aren't thinking about the effect their words could have.

Watch for an opportunity to speak to the person sometime when he's by himself. Remind him of the incident and tell him that you were hurt by it. Explain to him that using stereotypes to make fun of anyone's race or religion or ethnic background is wrong. It can cause misunderstanding, hurt feelings, and even hatred. And the next time something like this happens, be prepared to say something right then and there. Most teens are highly sensitive about their own feelings and will be able to tune into yours.

The Origins of Anti-Semitism

Anti-Semitism goes back to the time of the emergence of Christianity, when Jews were alleged to be responsible for the death of Christ and were criticized for rejecting Christianity.

Characterized as arrogant and bigoted, the Jews became the scapegoats (or convenient objects of blame) for many of the problems of daily life. Isolated and prohibited from owning land, they often became city dwellers and involved in commerce. They soon earned a reputation for being greedy and without morals.

Jewish teens, like this boy on the left, are sensitive to statements made out of prejudice or based on stereotypes. Think about it. Have you ever made a prejudiced remark that could have hurt some person? Putting yourself in that person's shoes may help stop you from doing it again.

As time went on, the Jews in Eastern Europe and Russia were forced to live in special areas, often poor and rural, and were subject to all kinds of restrictions in their daily lives. Until the early 20th century, waves of anti-Jewish feeling swept across Eastern Europe periodically. Armies attacked Jewish settlements, destroyed property, and murdered thousands of residents in raids called pogroms.

Hitler and the "Final Solution"

In the 20th century, anti-Jewish feeling intensified, especially in Germany during the years after World War I. At that time, Germany was suffering economically. It had never recovered from its severe defeat in the war. Many Germans had no money, no jobs, and not enough to eat. Adolf Hitler, who became chancellor of Germany in 1933, and his Nazi party played on the nation's hatred, anger, and shame. Through inflammatory speeches, he convinced many Germans that internal "enemies" had caused Germany's downfall. Heading Hitler's list of "enemies" were the Jews.

Hitler accused Jews of all sorts of crimes against the country, including the hoarding of wealth. He claimed that Jews were an "impure race" that was inferior to the "ideal German race," which he called "Aryan." Aryans, as defined by Hitler, were blond, blue-eyed, and vigorously healthy.

To create "a pure race of Aryans," Hitler devised his "final solution"—the annihilation of the Jews and other "impure" peoples, including gypsies, mentally and physically disabled people, homosexuals, and political opponents. The Nazis began rounding up such people and sending them to concentration camps.

Hitler tried to lead his so-called "master race" to world domination, and World War II resulted. As Hitler succeeded in conquering other European countries, his Nazi troops rounded up the nation's Jews and placed them in concentration camps, where they worked until they died, starved to death, or were systematically shot or killed in gas chambers.

There were few survivors. Before Hitler was finally defeated in 1945, he had succeeded in killing 6 million Jews—most of the Jewish population of Europe.

Anti-Semitism in America

Jews living in the United States have not had to undergo pogroms, confinement, or death in concentration camps. However, there is a long history of anti-Semitism in the country.

Origins

Though a few Jews settled in America during colonial times, the first Jews to come in numbers came in the 1850s and were from Germany. They were middle-class, educated, and industrious, and, despite being targets of prejudice for being both foreign and non-Christian, some made great fortunes in business and banking in the United States. After the 1880s, a great wave of poor, oppressed, rural Jews from Eastern Europe arrived. They were looking for a better life and safety from persecution. These people were culturally much different from the earlier immigrant group. The newer immigrants did not try to fit into the general population so easily. They attracted attention in America, both for their foreign manner and their religious fervor.

How It Worked

This new wave of Jewish people arrived at a time when "nativist" (or antiforeign) feeling was rampant among Americans. The Jews represented a threat to many Americans who resented not only their religion but also their soon-found social and economic success.

Anti-Semitic stereotypes appeared in the popular press and literature, and discriminatory practices appeared in housing, education, business, and social organizations.

■ Quotas restricted the number of Jews accepted in many colleges, universities, and professional schools.

■ Residential restrictions prevented Jews from owning property in many upper-class areas of the country through the use of a so-called "restrictive covenant" in real estate deeds. When someone bought a property in an area where Jews were not welcome, the buyer's lease included a clause stating that the property would not be resold to Jews. (Blacks, Asians, Italians, and many other minorities could also be excluded by restrictive covenants.)

■ Jews were discriminated against in many areas of employment, from semiskilled factory work to professional and commercial occupations.

■ Social organizations, country clubs, and resorts often excluded Jews entirely.

Discrimination Subsides

Following World War II, when Americans fully comprehended the horror of Hitler's anti-Semitism and its consequences, discrimination against Jews began to subside. Organizations like the Anti-Defamation League and the American Friends Service Committee conducted extensive educational campaigns to make the public more aware of these more subtle aspects of racism. And eventually, restrictive covenants and similar tactics that bar Jews, blacks, and other minorities from housing and other opportunities were declared unconstitutional.

Anti-Semitism Today

Unfortunately, anti-Semitism still exists in both Europe and America. In Germany, groups of neo-Nazis have formed over the last 50 years. They harass Jews and other minorities, and their activities have often led to violence and sometimes deaths.

In the United States, too, several neo-Nazi groups have formed since World War II. The original American Nazi Party, founded by George Lincoln Rockwell, advocated killing Jews and sending blacks to Africa. Following Rockwell's death in 1967, several descendant groups—such as the New Order and the National Alliance—were formed, but they have attracted few members.

Skinheads

More visible are the so-called "skinheads," who originated in England in the 1970s. The skinheads are gangs of belligerent, young whites who preach Nazi-like white supremacy and hatred of both Jews and blacks. They are known for their shaved heads, use of Nazi symbols, and their steel-toed boots, which they often use as weapons with which to kick their opponents. The National Council of Churches has reported that skinheads were responsible for more than 100 brutal killings and hundreds more assaults and cross-burnings in the mid-1980s alone.

Skinheads are one of the most vicious hate groups in America. Small numbers place them on society's fringe, but their hatred of Jews and African Americans has won them attention in the media.

So while anti-Semitic prejudice has decreased over the past decades, some hate groups are still at work making use of Jewish stereotypes and advocating violence. The Anti-Defamation League's annual report issued in January 1994 told of 1,876 anti-Semitic incidents occurring nationwide in 1993, the second highest number in the survey's 15-year history.

Some incidents reported in *The New York Times:*

■ In July 1993, an undercover investigation in Orange County, California, ended with ten arrests. Among them were leaders of the Fourth Reich Skinheads, who admitted to making bombs for criminal acts. Planned acts included the bombing of a black church and attacks on synagogues.

■ In July 1993, two students were arrested for painting anti-Semitic messages on the Commack (L.I.) High School athletic field on graduation day in June.

■ In September 1993, three teenage boys were arrested in Saddle Brook, New Jersey, and accused of spray-painting swastikas and pro-Hitler slogans on 98 tombstones.

The Denial of the Holocaust

One of the saddest and most insidious forms of anti-Semitism is the allegation that the Holocaust (the killing of the Jews by Hitler's Nazis during World War II) never happened. Aimed at the generation who did not live through that period of history, this rumor has gained strength and is being repeated irresponsibly in many quarters. Anti-Semitism has been called "the disease that won't die," and the denial of the Holocaust is surely one of the most terrible symptoms of that disease.

CHAPTER 5

Fear and Violence

Q There seems to be so much trouble between races, like fighting and riots. Rap singers are angry and threatening, gangs fight each other, people get hurt and killed. Why? It scares me.

A Racial violence has been reported in the news media a lot recently. That may be because it is getting wider coverage since the Rodney King beating in 1991. But racial violence, like racism, has been around a long time.

Violence and the Ku Klux Klan

You can't talk about racial violence without mentioning the notorious Ku Klux Klan. The Klan, or KKK, was founded in the South after the Civil War to keep white people in power. Disguising their identities in white sheets and hoods, the original Klan members led raids into black communities, terrorizing residents, dragging people from their homes, whipping or beating them, destroying property, and sometimes lynching people. Many southern whites sympathized with the Klan, if not with their methods, and most were intimidated. Law enforcement was often impossible.

The 20th-Century Klan

Membership declined in the Klan by the early 20th century, but rising racial tensions in the North after World War I led to the Klan's rebirth in the 1920s. The Klan claimed a membership of 3 million all across the country at that time.

The later Klan was also anti-Semitic, anti-Catholic, and anti-immigrant. It was against communists and other radicals, and labor unions. Today, more than 50 different Klan groups operate, many outside of the South. The largest group, known as The Invisible Empire, Knights of the KKK, has its headquarters in Connecticut and boasts 2,000 members.

The Rodney King Case

In sharp contrast to the disguised night raids of the Klan, in March 1991, Rodney King, a black motorist, was stopped on a public thoroughfare by white Los Angeles police for speeding and then severely beaten. The beating was videotaped by a passerby and shown on television across the country thousands of times. People responded with outrage to what appeared to be a savage and unprovoked attack. Four policemen were indicted on charges that included assault with a deadly weapon and inflicting bodily injury. A year later, a jury refused to convict the policemen on all but one minor charge.

Riots!

In protest of the verdict, violence broke out in minority areas of Los Angeles. Vandalism and looting were widespread. Pedestrians were attacked. Fires burned out of control. When the riots finally ended three days later, 52 people were dead, thousands were injured and arrested, and property damage was estimated in the millions.

Obviously blacks were enraged at what seemed to them—and to many whites, too—a miscarriage of justice. In 1993, the four policemen were tried on federal charges of violating King's civil rights. Two were found guilty by this second jury, but they are appealing the verdict. Meanwhile, the black community is closely following the progress of the Rodney King case. Many blacks say that police abuse of minorities is commonplace, and they fear that it will continue.

Behind the Riots

Because of the riots, many poor areas in Los Angeles suffered large amounts of damage. Entire neighborhoods were burned down, and it will probably be years before they can be completely rebuilt. But the King beating alone did not trigger this outpouring of violence. Minority rage had been building in Los Angeles for years.

Unemployment

A major source of tension in Los Angeles and other cities with a large minority population is unemployment. Unemployment rates among African Americans, especially young, black men, have risen dramatically in the last decade. Nearly half of all black men between the ages of 16 and 19 who are in the labor force do not have jobs.

Throughout history, unemployment—and its effect on living standards—has created tension and violence. In the inner cities, unemployment is linked to a high crime rate. When unemployment is experienced by discontented people who believe they are victims of racial persecution, it is not surprising that violent outbursts occur. This kind of senseless violence then creates feelings of fear and distrust against minorities.

Unrest at Colleges

These feelings are not directed only to minority neighborhoods. Almost daily, television, magazines, and newspapers bring viewers and readers reports of racial "incidents" in various communities. One place where racial discontent appears to be increasing is on college campuses. Black students and white students are at a standoff, leading almost separate lives, and Asians are often resented for their academic achievement and their ever-increasing presence at universities. Racial tensions at these educational institutions reflect problems and divisions in society at large.

Black Racism

The subjects of race and violence have also begun to enter popular culture. Several popular rap singers comment on the current racial situation in their songs. A group called *Public Enemy,* for example, uses rap to talk about the exploitation of black labor and culture by whites, inner city anger, and fear of violence. Ice T (known for his song "Cop Killer") and Ice Cube are so-called "gangsta rappers," who describe the plight of the inner city dwellers, use rough expressions, and tease with their lyrics. Though rap singers deny it, many people say that rappers incite violence.

Sister Soljah

In an incident involving Bill Clinton when he was a candidate for the presidency in 1992, rap singer Sister Soljah was accused of being a black racist, and of inciting violence. Following the Los Angeles riots, Sister Soljah was quoted in an interview in *The Washington Post* as saying, "If black people kill black people every day, why not have a week and kill white people." To Clinton and to others, her statement seemed to justify the acts of the black youths who participated in the burning and looting of Los Angeles and also seemed to invite further killing.

Ice Cube, one of the so-called "gangsta rappers," is popular among teens. The lyrics written by rap musicians often include images of the violence and poverty found in American cities today.

Clinton Responds

Clinton was invited by the Reverend Jesse Jackson to speak at a meeting of his Rainbow Coalition in Washington, D.C., in June 1992, where Sister Soljah was also speaking. Clinton criticized Sister Soljah, thereby offending Jesse Jackson, who felt attacked as host. Sister Soljah said Clinton misinterpreted her comments and took them out of context. She said they were not intended literally but were meant to convey an attitude of gang members. She has also said that she can't be a black racist, because there is no such thing—blacks don't have power over whites. The controversy went on for months during the presidential campaign.

Farrakhan

In recent years, Louis Farrakhan, the head of the Nation of Islam, has made inflammatory anti-Semitic speeches on college campuses. The Nation of Islam, a separatist black religious organization whose members are called Black Muslims, preaches black supremacy. The organization was originally founded in 1930 by Elijah Muhammed, whose chief disciple was Malcolm X. The organization has a broad appeal to poor inner-city blacks because it stresses black pride. Supporters of the Nation of Islam are proud that it has helped many blacks.

Before Malcolm X was murdered by blacks in 1964, he had renounced his hatred of whites and begun to work toward the reconciliation of both races. After Malcolm X's death (many think Farrakhan was responsible for it), Farrakhan, who was originally recruited by Malcolm, restored the original Nation of Islam and refused to work with whites.

Farrakhan's Message

The Nation of Islam teaches that all white people are "devils." It calls upon members to confront whites and Jews, who are believed by Black Muslims to be the enemies of blacks. In 1985, a *Chicago Sun Times* reporter quoted Farrakhan as referring to Judaism as a "gutter religion." Farrakhan said that was a distortion of his words. But he maintained that some Jews have profited from the condition of African Americans. Denounced by leaders of both the Republican and Democratic parties, Farrakhan said, "If the United States government continues to submit to the Jewish lobby, it will lead the nation to its total destruction."

Reactions

Many people, both black and white, dislike Farrakhan's racist speeches. They are dismayed by his use of false statements to arouse anger and incite violence by blacks against whites. Among other charges, Farrakhan has outwardly accused Jewish scientists of creating the AIDS virus to destroy the black race. He also charges that black people are being killed by white doctors so that their organs can be "harvested" for use in transplant operations.

Nonetheless, the National Association for the Advancement of Colored People (NAACP), one of the least militant of all groups, invited Farrakhan to come in 1994 to a summit meeting of all black organizations. The invitation was regretted by many blacks and whites alike, who objected to providing such serious consideration of Farrakhan's racist views. And the meeting has caused much controversy within the NAACP.

***New York Times* Poll**

In March 1994, The New York Times found in a poll of African Americans that:

- 15% agreed with a statement saying that Farrakhan represented the views of most blacks in America.

- 40% disagreed with the statement.

- 66% agreed with a statement saying that most whites feel they are superior to blacks.

■ 40% agreed with a statement saying that most Jews are against progress by blacks.

■ 32% agreed with a statement saying that most white people want to keep blacks down.

■ 23% agreed with a statement saying it is true that the government deliberately makes sure that drugs are available in poor black neighborhoods in order to harm black people.

Minorities vs. Minorities

Minority hatred of other minorities is not new, but its incidence appears to be growing. Several recent studies have shown that minority prejudice against other minorities is greater than white dislike of any single minority group.

■ In addition to black anti-Semitism, black attacks on Hispanics have been reported. Some inner-city blacks claim that newly arrived immigrants from Latin America are taking jobs from them.

■ Tensions between blacks and Asians who operate stores in black neighborhoods have also erupted in violence. Blacks accuse Asian merchants of treating them with contempt and even assaulting them. The Asians say they fear black crime and the destruction of their stores.

Overcoming Violence

Fortunately, many people are working to overcome racism and hate. The Anti-Defamation League, a Jewish human rights organization, is cooperating with African American groups like the NAACP to work for greater understanding between blacks and Jews. The League is trying to establish an ongoing dialogue with blacks through community-based activities.

Overcoming racism remains a goal for all young people today. As America becomes more and more diverse, it will be necessary to find ways to live together in harmony.

Many Jews have long been supporters of black civil rights and were active as both leaders and participants in the U.S. civil rights movement of the 1960s. In 1992 the Jewish Museum of New York and the NAACP set up a joint traveling exhibit, "Bridges and Boundaries." The exhibit chronicles the persecution of both blacks and Jews, as well as the many efforts that Jews have made on behalf of black rights. It seems appropriate that the final stop of "Bridges and Boundaries" occurred in 1994 in Chicago—the home of the Nation of Islam.

Understanding the Source of Racism

Q I guess I just have a hard time understanding where all this racism comes from. Is there no solution to it?

A The sources of racism—bias, discrimination, and violence—are many and complex. Sometimes racism can take the form of a word, a look, or a thoughtless action;

other times it comes from years of history and custom. While no one has yet found a solution to racism in the United States, we must learn to understand that we are a country of many peoples who are dependent upon one another, and if we remain divided, we shall surely fall apart.

Let's review, then, some of the sources of racism we have talked about.

■ Racism can start at home with the views of our parents or an older generation. Share your own feelings with your family and try to understand theirs. Stick up for what you believe.

■ The desire to belong to a group—particularly during the teenage years—can often lead to the separation of races and to misunderstandings. Offer friendship to other groups and learn all you can about them.

■ Using or repeating stereotypes is one of the most dangerous pitfalls of racism. Think about what you are saying and avoid making generalizations.

■ Learn all that you can about the history of racism in America in order to better understand the deeply ingrained feelings of all peoples.

■ Take stock of your own attitudes, beliefs, and behavior concerning race, and eliminate all of the prejudices, stereotypes, and misconceptions.

■ Finally, have a firm commitment to the principles of equality and a respect for each individual and for group differences. The transfer of this commitment from person to person throughout the world can be our only sure hope for an honorable and peaceful future.

CHAPTER 6

Fighting Discrimination

Q My dad's really down on affirmative action and hiring quotas. He's not a racist or anything like that, but he's really tired of being passed over for promotion. He says they're always promoting minorities, even if they aren't qualified. Do you think he's right to feel sore about it?

A It's understandable that your dad is irritated and disappointed if he's not moving ahead in his job. He might want to discuss the situation with his supervisor to find out where he really stands. Many people have had to make difficult adjustments under the new quota hiring practices, but they should at least understand the reasons why the practices came about and what purposes they serve.

• • • • • • • • • • • •

Affirmative action is a policy, supported by law, that attempts to make up for previous hiring practices that restricted the participation of blacks and other minorities in the work force. Under affirmative action, companies must set aside a certain percentage of places for minority employees. Companies must also provide sufficient opportunities for minority promotions. If affirmative action guidelines cannot be met, companies must be able to prove to the governmental agency that they made a serious effort to fulfill them.

Affirmative action is not confined to hiring practices.

Universities and colleges must also follow affirmative action guidelines in deciding which students to admit.

Affirmative action programs became necessary because discrimination was continuing despite the passage of civil rights laws guaranteeing free access to both jobs and education. Unwritten policies silently kept many minorities, especially blacks, out of major companies and schools, or restricted their numbers according to "gentleman's agreement" quotas. Affirmative action encourages minorities to apply for jobs and for school admission, and then guarantees that a certain percentage of them will be accepted.

Success—and Failure

There is no doubt that affirmative action has opened the doors of companies and universities to many minorities. To take the example of African Americans, better education and wider employment opportunities in turn have increased the number of black teachers, social workers, accountants, and business managers. Affirmative action has also helped raise the standard of living for many blacks. The median income of black married-couple families grew to 83 percent of that of comparable white families.

However, other statistics are not so encouraging. According to the 1990 census, in 1989 the per capita income of $8,850 was lower than the national per capita income of $14,140; and the median income for all black families had risen from about $21,110 in 1979 to only $22,430 in 1989.

So, affirmative action has not been an overwhelming success. Despite increased opportunities for higher education created by affirmative action programs, fewer blacks are graduating from college. There is a corresponding decline in the number of blacks going on to postgraduate education.

The black unemployment rate, which was twice that of whites 30 years ago, has increased even further. There are still relatively few blacks in many professions, especially those that are science-related. And despite new hiring practices, there are very few blacks in the highest executive levels of corporations.

Reverse Discrimination?

Not everyone approves of affirmative action. Many white men believe that affirmative action policies have discriminated against *them.* They charge that affirmative action has really created what they call *reverse discrimination.*

Many lawsuits have been filed that challenge the legality of affirmative action on the basis of reverse discrimination. Some have been settled on the side of minorities, while others have been settled in favor of those claiming reverse discrimination.

One of the most famous cases concerning affirmative action and a claim of reverse discrimination occurred in the mid-1970s. A white student named Allan Bakke sued the University of California medical school, claiming that he had been denied admission in favor of less-qualified minority applicants. Bakke's case was finally decided by the U.S. Supreme Court in his favor.

Critics of affirmative action believe that the policy helps less-qualified workers to receive promotions while passing over those who are better qualified. White students sometimes complain that under affirmative action, minorities with lower grade point averages and standardized test scores keep them from attending their first-choice colleges.

Defending Affirmative Action

Undoubtedly, under affirmative action many qualified whites have been passed over in favor of less-qualified minority students. However, in response to this criticism, minorities say that they deserve special treatment for past injustices.

They and other defenders of affirmative action also say that less-qualified whites have enjoyed special advantages for years. This, they say, was true in many major companies,

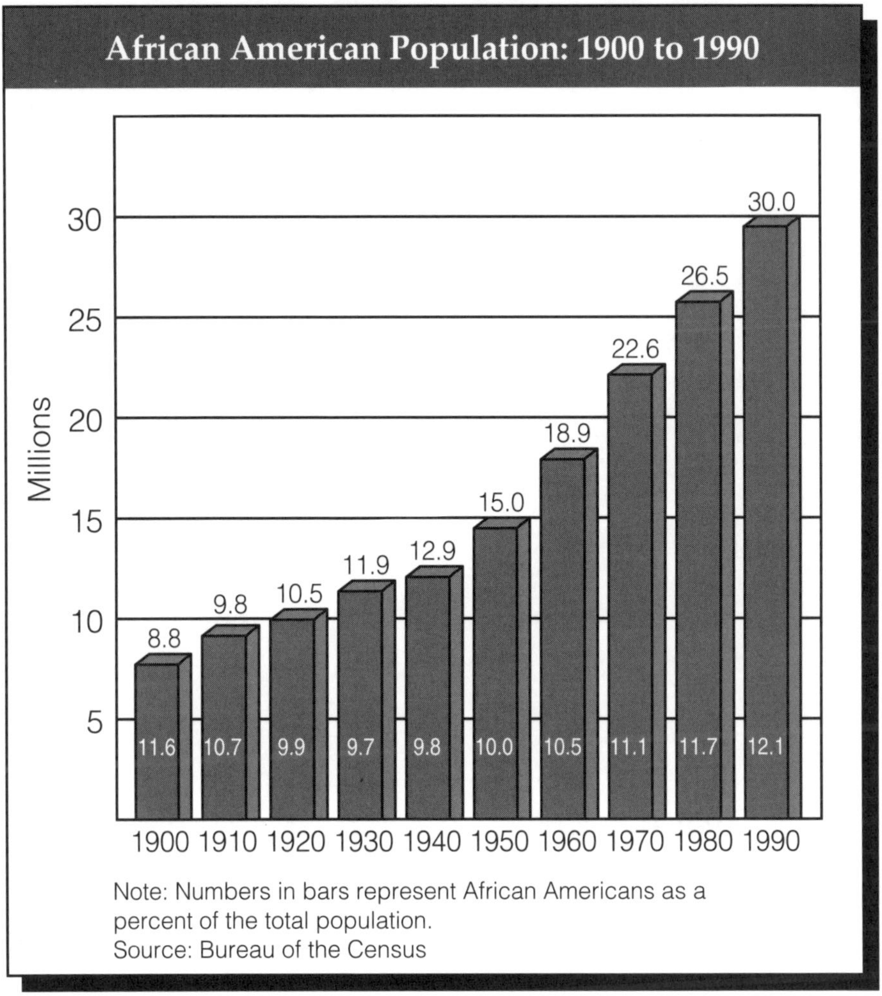

where minorities were only hired for menial positions.

Defenders of affirmative action also say that for many years whites have enjoyed an advantage in college and university admissions. In the past, many top educational institutions traditionally admitted mediocre white students, in particular sons and daughters of alumni.

Some educators also believe that standardized tests have been unfair to minority students. Low scores by minorities, say these educators, are not an accurate reflection of minority abilities. Furthermore, minority students may have attended inferior elementary and high schools, where their potential was not developed.

Finally, many people believe that affirmative action benefits society as a whole, because it helps to ensure that the abilities and skills of all members of society will be maximized.

Minorities and Affirmative Action

Despite these voices of support for affirmative action, many minority leaders, especially blacks, do not like the policy. They say that affirmative action is insulting to the people that it is trying to help.

One such critic was the late tennis star Arthur Ashe. "I would not want to know that I received a job simply because I am black," Ashe wrote shortly before his death in 1993. "What I and others want is an equal chance, under one set of rules."

Equalizing Opportunity

Affirmative action is not the only policy designed to give blacks and other minorities a helping hand. Federal and state government agencies administer job-training programs that favor minorities. Another well-known antidiscrimination program in the United States is school busing.

Because of continued patterns of segregation in housing—there are still entire neighborhoods and communities where one race overwhelmingly predominates—U.S. schools have not been fully integrated in compliance with the Supreme Court ruling of 1954. In the 1960s, federal courts began ordering school officials to provide buses to take pupils to other school districts in order to achieve racial diversity.

Busing, like affirmative action, has been bitterly opposed. Many people do not believe that small children should be forced to attend schools far from their neighborhoods. On the other hand, defenders of busing believe this is the only way that many children will get to know people of different races and ethnic groups. In the long run, they say, busing will create racial harmony.

Affirmative action, preferential job-training programs, busing, and other attempts to right the many past wrongs done to minorities continue to be challenged in the courts. At some future date these programs may be eliminated entirely because of opposition both from the white population and from the very minorities that they are intended to help.

Busing children to other school districts to improve racial diversity is also sometimes controversial. The children on this bus, however, may have no other opportunity to experience people different from themselves.

What You Can Do

Affirmative action is a very complicated issue that is inadequately understood. Many white critics of affirmative action programs, for example, don't know that many minorities oppose them, too. And supporters of such programs often do not explain fully the ways in which they have undeniably benefited many minority group members.

But the biggest problem with affirmative action may be that not enough people realize why such a policy is needed in the first place. Many people assume that civil rights laws have made life completely better for blacks and other minorities.

Q I think I'm beginning to understand more about affirmative action now. And I don't think my father should be so sore about it. But what can I do?

A Talk to your father about affirmative action. Explain to him that many minorities have known discrimination for so long that they think they're entitled to compensation, even if it looks like reverse discrimination. To learn what you can about affirmative action policies:

■ Ask your social studies teacher and your school guidance counselor how to find out more about affirmative action and its effect on your community.

■ Do local schools bus their students to other districts to achieve racial integration?

■ Are minority students applying to and being accepted at colleges around the country?

■ Do white students in your high school believe that minorities are given priority in college admissions or in job-training programs?

Learning more about these programs and discussing them with your friends and classmates may help ease racial tensions.

Can We All Get Along?

In the end, there can be only one goal in our multiracial society. It was expressed by Rodney King after the Los Angeles riots of 1992. "Can we all get along?" King pleaded.

The potential for getting along is certainly there. In a 1993 poll of all races and ethnic groups, an overwhelming majority—81 percent—expressed the belief that relations among races can be improved. In addition, a 1993 survey of college newspaper editors revealed that 88 percent of them believe it is possible to improve race relations on their campuses.

So do your part and make it happen.

Where to Go for Help

School counselors, social studies teachers, and your school librarian can help you learn more about racism. Clergy at your church or synagogue may also be able to provide you with useful information and advice on how to handle racism in your daily life.

In addition, many communities have established human rights commissions as part of their local government. These commissions investigate complaints of racism in their respective communities. If your community has a human rights commission, visit it for information on its activities and find out how its members can help you—and how you can help them.

The following organizations are dedicated to eliminating racism in our society. Write to them for more information on their activities. Some of them, like the American Friends Service Committee, have antiracism projects in which you and your school may be able to participate.

American Civil Liberties Union
132 West 43rd Street
New York, NY 10036

American Friends Service Committee
1501 Cherry Street
Philadelphia, PA 19102

Anti-Defamation League of B'nai B'rith
823 United Nations Plaza
New York, NY 10017

Center for Democratic Renewal
P.O. Box 50469
Atlanta, GA 30302

Congress of Racial Equality (CORE)
1457 Flatbush Avenue
Brooklyn, NY 11210

Martin Luther King Center for Nonviolent Social Change
449 Auburn Avenue NE
Atlanta, GA 30312

National Association for the Advancement of Colored People (NAACP)
4805 Mt. Hope Drive
Baltimore, MD 21215

National Urban League
500 E. 62nd Street
New York, NY 10021

Simon Wiesenthal Center/The Museum of Tolerance
9670 W. Pico Boulevard
Los Angeles, CA 90035

Tales, Inc.
R.R. 2, Box 401
Urbana, IL 61801

Where to Go for Help

Canadian Alliance in Solidarity with Native Peoples
39 Spadina Rd., Lower Level
Toronto, ON MSR 259
(416) 972-1573

Canadian Centre on Racism and Prejudices
C.P. 505, Suce Desjardins
Montreal, QC H5B 1B6
(514) 727-2936

Canadian Council on Human Rights & Race Relations
The Guardian Tower, #1506
141 Adelaide St. W.
Toronto, ON M5H 3L5
(416) 594-3291

Centre for Research-Action on Race Relations (CRARR)
220-1650 Rue Berri
Montreal QC H2C4E6
(514) 843-3892

Kids Help Phone (Canada)
#100 – 2Bloor St. W.
P.O. Box 513
Toronto, ON M4W 3E2
1-800-668-6868

Minority Advocacy & Rights Council Foundation (Canada)
#1100, 251 Laurier Ave, W.
Ottawa, ON KIP 5J6

For More Information

An asterisk (*) indicates a book geared specifically toward young adults.

Nonfiction

Allport, Gordon. *The Nature of Prejudice*. Addison-Wesley, 1954.

Ashe, Arthur, and Arnold Rampersad. *Days of Grace*. Knopf, 1993.

The Autobiography of Malcolm X (with the assistance of Alex Haley). Grove Press, 1965.

Brown, Dee. *Bury My Heart at Wounded Knee*. Holt, Rinehart, 1974.

Cleaver, Eldridge. *Soul on Ice*. McGraw-Hill, 1968.

Coon, Carleton S. *The Origin of Races*. Knopf, 1962.

Delany, Sarah and Elizabeth A., with Amy Hill Hearth, *Having Our Say: The Delany Sisters' First Hundred Years*. Kodansha, 1993.

Du Bois, W. E. B. *The Souls of Black Folk*. NAL-Dutton, 1969.

Frank, Anne. *The Diary of a Young Girl*. Franklin Watts, 1952.

Glazer, Nathan, and Daniel Patrick Moynihan. *The Melting Pot*. MIT Press, 1970.

Hate Groups in America. Anti-Defamation League of B'nai B'rith, 1988.

Hundley, Norris, Jr., ed. *The Asian American: The Historical Experience*. Clio Books, 1976.

Jackson, Helen Hunt. *A Century of Dishonor*. Scholarly, 1972.

Johnson, James Weldon. *Autobiography of an Ex-Colored Man*. Viking Penguin, 1990.

*Kronenwetter, Michael. *United They Hate: White Supremacist Groups in America*. Walker & Co., 1992.

For More Information

*Langone, John. *Spreading Poison: A Book About Racism and Prejudice*. Little, Brown, 1993.

Meier, Matt S., and Feliciano Rivera, eds. *Readings on La Raza: A Collection of Essays about Mexican-Americans*. Hill & Wang, 1974.

Moutoussamy-Ashe, Jeanne. *Daddy and Me: A Photo Story of Arthur Ashe and His Daughter, Camera*. Knopf, 1993.

*Pascoe, Elaine. *Racial Prejudice*. Franklin Watts, 1985.

Staples, Brent. *Parallel Time*. Pantheon Books, 1994.

Washington, Booker T. *Up from Slavery*. Viking Penguin, 1986.

Wright, Richard. *Black Boy*. Harper & Row, 1945.

Fiction

Baldwin, James. *Go Tell It on the Mountain*. Knopf, 1953.

Ellison, Ralph. *Invisible Man*. Random House, 1952.

Gaines, Ernest J. *The Autobiography of Miss Jane Pitman*. Dial, 1971.

*Herlihy, Dirlie. *Ludie's Song*. Dial, 1988.

Hobson, Laura Z. *Gentleman's Agreement*. Simon & Schuster, 1947. (See also listing under "Movies," below.)

Jackson, Helen Hunt. *Ramona*. NAL-Dutton, 1988.

*Taylor, Mildred. *Roll of Thunder, Hear My Cry*. Dial, 1976.

Films

Come See the Paradise, 1990 (prejudice against Japanese Americans).

Gentleman's Agreement, 1947 (anti-Semitism).

Guess Who's Coming to Dinner?, 1967 (prejudice against African Americans).

Malcolm X, 1993 (biography of the Black Muslim leader).

Schindler's List, 1993 (anti-Semitism in Hitler's Germany).

INDEX